For my friends,
whether near or far

SIMON & SCHUSTER BOOKS FOR YOUNG READERS
An imprint of Simon & Schuster Children's Publishing Division
1230 Avenue of the Americas, New York, New York 10020
Copyright © 2020 by Chris Naylor-Ballesteros
Originally published in Great Britain in 2020 by Nosy Crow Ltd.
First US edition 2021
All rights reserved, including the right of reproduction in whole or in part in any form.
SIMON & SCHUSTER BOOKS FOR YOUNG READERS is a trademark of Simon & Schuster, Inc.
For information about special discounts for bulk purchases, please contact Simon & Schuster
Special Sales at 1-866-506-1949 or business@simonandschuster.com.
The Simon & Schuster Speakers Bureau can bring authors to your live event.
For more information or to book an event, contact the Simon & Schuster Speakers
Bureau at 1-866-248-3049 or visit our website at www.simonspeakers.com.
The text for this book was set in Filosofia OT.
Manufactured in China · 1220 NOS
10 9 8 7 6 5 4 3 2 1
Library of Congress Cataloging-in-Publication Data
Names: Naylor-Ballesteros, Chris, author, illustrator.
Title: Out of nowhere / Chris Naylor-Ballesteros.
Description: First edition. | New York : Simon & Schuster, [2021] | Originally published: London :
Nosy Crow Ltd, 2020. | Audience: Ages 4-8. | Audience: Grades K-1. | Summary: A beetle courageously sets
out in search of his best friend—a caterpillar that arrived out of nowhere and vanished without warning.
Identifiers: LCCN 2020012082 | ISBN 9781534481008 (hardcover) | ISBN 9781534481015 (eBook)
Subjects: CYAC: Best friends—Fiction. | Friendship—Fiction. | Beetles—Fiction. | Caterpillars—Fiction. |
Metamorphosis—Fiction. | Butterflies—Fiction.
Classification: LCC PZ7.1.N376 Out 2021 | DDC [E]—dc23
LC record available at https://lccn.loc.gov/2020012082

Out of Nowhere

CHRIS NAYLOR-BALLESTEROS

Simon & Schuster Books for Young Readers

New York   London   Toronto   Sydney   New Delhi

Once, I had a friend.

She arrived out of nowhere one day.
I asked where she'd come from, but she just didn't know.

She stayed with me and, every day, we shared
a picnic on the big rock looking out over the forest.

Then, at the end of each day, we would watch the moon come up together.

But one morning, I woke up and my friend
was nowhere to be seen.

I looked everywhere . . .

. . . and at last!

There was my friend—lost,
deep in the forest.

Now, I know I look very strong with my tough
shell and spiky horns. The truth is, sometimes . . .

I don't feel very strong at all.
But if I wanted to find my friend, I'd just
have to pretend.

I packed a very big picnic and set off.

I sang a song to myself to feel a little bit stronger.

"I'm a beetle and don't you know?
I'm not afraid of a hungry crow.
Yes, I'm a beetle and can't you see?
Fearsome frogs don't frighten me.
Oh, I'm a beetle and, er . . . haven't you heard?
I'll keep singing till . . . till I run out of words!"

No one bothered me much, so I think it worked.

And then, just when my big brave song
finally ran out of words, I was there!

But I realized I'd made a very big mistake.

I had no idea where my friend was.

I was tired, and it was a very long way back to the big rock, so I decided to stay for a while.

Just until I got my strength back.

And then, out of nowhere,
someone suddenly arrived.

I felt as if I'd seen her before, but at first, I couldn't quite
put my finger on where.

Then I looked more closely. And I just knew.
It was my friend! She had changed a little bit,
but it was my friend all the same.

We shared my picnic, just like before.

We did the same the day after.
And the day after that.

And today too.
It's just like before, on the big rock.

Then, at the end of each day, we take off
to watch the moon come up together.

And my friend is with me again.

Out of nowhere.